AMADITO
AND
SPIDER WOMAN

Library of Congress Cataloging-in-Publication pending

Design by Bob Jivanjee
Prepress: Ali Graphic Services Inc.
Printed in Hong Kong.

9 8 7 6 5 4 3 2

Kiva Publishing
Walnut, CA

*To my mother
and her great-grandson Derick
with special thanks to Todd*

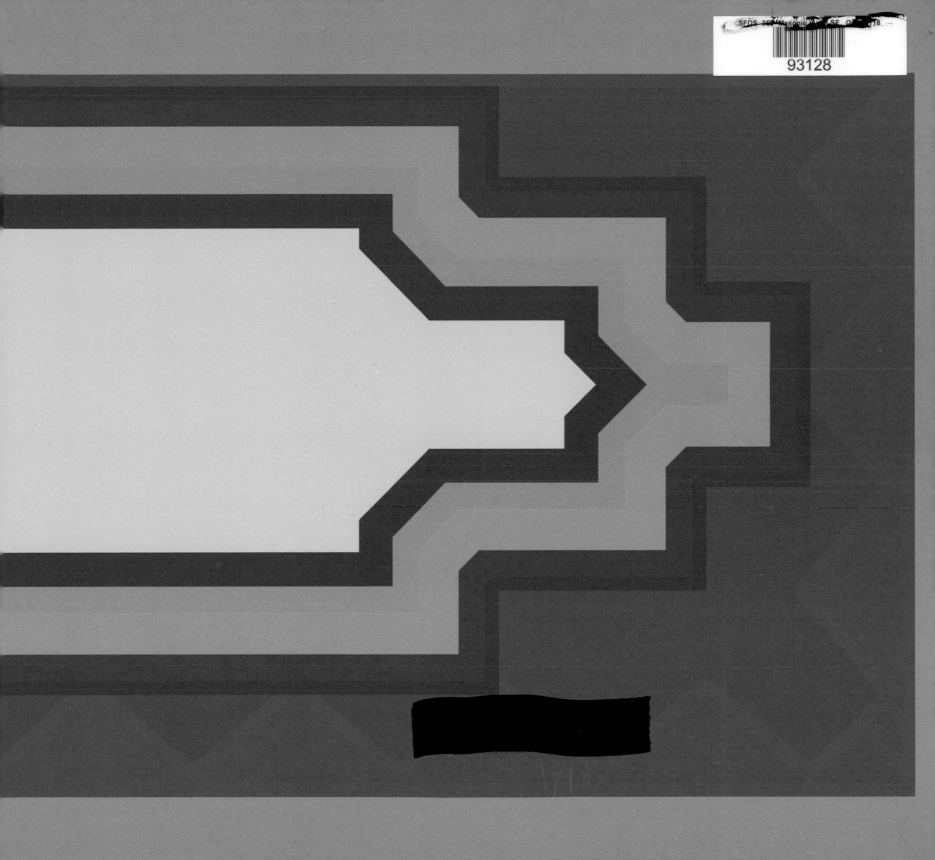

AMADITO
AND
SPIDER WOMAN

by Lisa Bear Goldman • Illustrated by Amado M. Peña, Jr.

KIVA
PUBLISHING, INC.

When Amadito opened the door to his home, he saw his mother busy chopping vegetables. The warm smells of green chili stew and dinner greeted him. Amadito's brother, Diego, sat at the table braiding new leather reins for his horse. Amadito's grandmother, whom he called Nana, sat where she often sat, weaving a beautiful thick blanket on her loom. On another day Amadito's heart would have been filled with joy.

"What is the matter, Amadito? Have you been crying?" Mama asked.

Amadito nodded. "A kid made fun of me in front of the class today."

Mama walked away from her cooking and gave him a hug. "I am sorry. You are a good boy, Amadito. Remember that. I have lots of work to do to get dinner ready. Now do your chores and you will feel better." Amadito watched her walk back to the stove where she stirred the stew. Mama had her serious working face on.

Amadito took out the trash. He fed the chickens and watered the dogs. He even did his homework. But he did not feel better. The pain and heavy feeling in his chest were still there.

Diego, his brother, looked up from the table where he worked. "I'll tell you what you need to do."

Amadito knew Diego had the answers to many questions, so he listened carefully.

Diego's words were strongly spoken, "Those kids are bullies. You have to get mad and let them know they can't push you around. That's the only way to take care of them." Diego slapped the leather hard on the table, and Amadito jumped in surprise with the loud and sharp sound it made.

Amadito thought hard about what Diego had said. He tried to feel the anger, and when he did, he made it grow. Amadito scowled and thought of all the things he'd like to do when he saw the kids again. But that sad, heavy feeling still found a home in his heart.

Amadito's father walked through the door. Amadito was surprised. He hadn't heard his truck on the road.

Papa stood in front of him looking bigger than usual in his work shirt, work boots, and large straw hat. He looked at Amadito with concern as he spoke. "Why are your eyes so angry, my son?"

Amadito told him what had happened and how he was trying to get rid of his hurt feelings.

After some thought, Papa spoke in his serious tone. "Son, you have to be tough sometimes. Don't let anyone hurt you. You must be strong."

Amadito wanted to be like Papa. He was a man the family, neighbors, and even strangers looked up to. People often came to him for advice. Amadito thought to himself, "I will build a strong wall around my heart and no one will ever hurt me."

Nana rose slowly from her loom. "Amadito, come help me gather plants for my dyes."

Amadito took her arm and they walked onto the mesa. The sun was low in the western sky, and the cholla cactus seemed to shine with their own bright light on the desert floor. Nana did not seem interested in gathering plants.

When they were far from the house, Nana said, "Come sit beside me." Amadito sat on a rock next to her, and they looked around in comfortable silence. A small spider crawled on the ground, and Nana placed her hand in front of it so that it crawled onto her finger. She smiled at the spider. Amadito knew Nana saw spiders as her friends. Her smile seemed to say she shared a wonderful secret with the spider.

"Aren't you afraid of spiders?" Amadito asked.

"Fear is our own creation," Nana said thoughtfully, "When one looks deep into the nature of a thing, fear usually disappears. It is also true that if there is peace within one's heart, fear can find no resting place inside us."

Amadito thought of the kids at school and wished he were not afraid of feeling hurt by them.

The sun was getting close to the top of the mesa, and Nana let the spider crawl away on the hard earth. She spoke in her gentle way. "Your feelings are a precious treasure inside you. Do not hide from them."

She gazed at the desert floor. "Look out there. The ants are still hard at work. They stay busy and never stop. Some people try to avoid pain in this way."

Nana pointed to the desert floor. "See how sharp and harsh the cactus is, my Grandson. Some people try to cover their pain with anger, and they become like the cactus."

Nana nodded toward a desert tortoise, slowly and clumsily making its way to cover. "Some people build a strong protection around their hearts just as the tortoise has his shell. They believe they can avoid feeling pain in this way."

"Do not be afraid of your feelings, Amadito," Nana whispered.

Amadito thought of his family and how they had tried to help him. He let himself feel his sadness, and a tear moved down his cheek.

Then he thought about all that she had said.

"How do you know these things, Nana?"

"It is a way of looking at the world around you. Look at the small things and then look at the whole. You will learn much about yourself and the world around you."

She wiped Amadito's tears away and looked toward the red and gold sunset.

"Keep your eyes open to the beauty and wonder of this world and keep your heart open. Miracles will come to you."

Nana said, "I am tired, my little one. I must go inside."

Amadito watched her walk back to their home. Although silence surrounded him, he did not feel alone. Amadito turned Nana's words around in his head and in his heart.

Stars began to appear. The more he gazed at them, the more stars he saw. He looked closely at the Big Dipper and the North Star. He then tried to look at the whole sky. He let the beauty of what he saw wash over him.

Amadito then knew he was part of this miracle and that the miracle was also inside him. He was a small part of the whole. A warm and gentle peace filled his heart. Amadito was comforted and there was no room for fear.

Amadito was happy.

He promised himself he would look at one thing a day in a different way. He would keep his eyes and his heart open, and maybe when he was as old as Nana, he would be as wise as she.

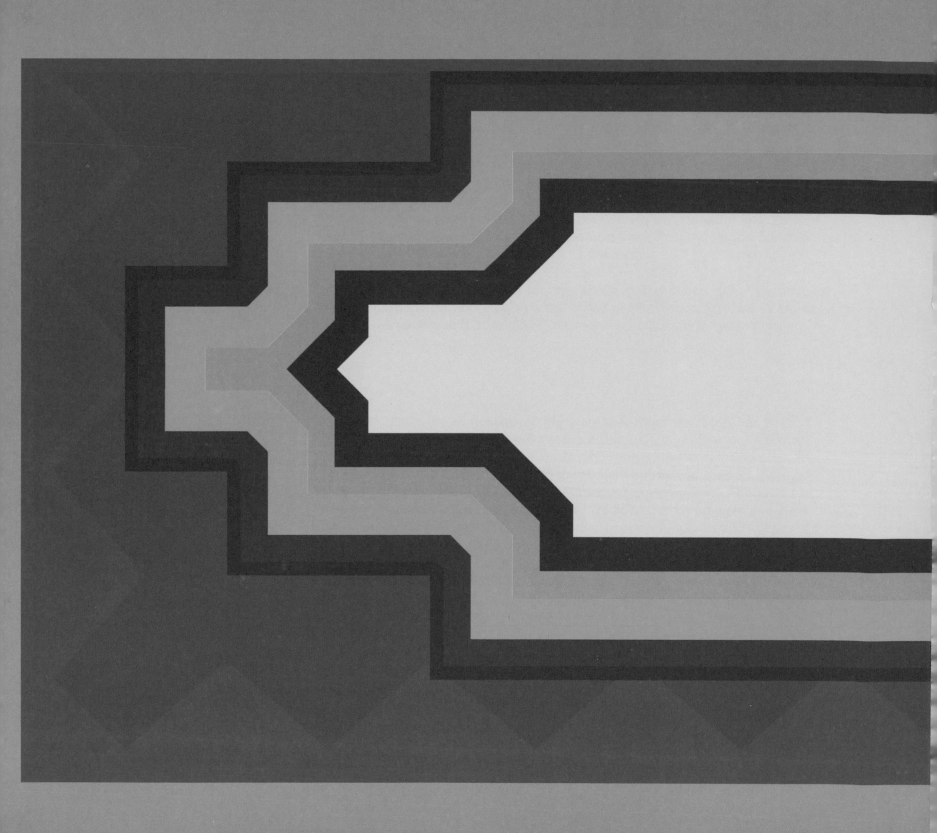